For Penny
D.M.

For Sophie Higgs
(a promise kept!)
D.G.

Text © 1993 by David Martin
Illustrations © 1993 by Debi Gliori

First edition 1993

Library of Congress Cataloging-in-Publication Data
Martin, David, 1944-
Lizzie and her friend / David Martin; illustrated by Debi Gliori. — 1st ed.
Summary: Lizzie and Penny have fun playing with water.
ISBN 1-56402-061-4
[1. Play — Fiction. 2. Stories in rhyme.]
I. Gliori, Debi, ill. II. Title
PZ8.3.M4115Lip 1993 92-53009
[E] — dc20

10 9 8 7 6 5 4 3 2 1

Printed in Hong Kong

The pictures for this book were done in watercolor.

Candlewick Press
2067 Massachusetts Avenue
Cambridge, Massachusetts 02140

Lizzie
and Her Friend

DAVID MARTIN

illustrated by
DEBI GLIORI

CANDLEWICK PRESS
CAMBRIDGE, MASSACHUSETTS

Where is Lizzie?
Lizzie's at the hose.

What is Lizzie doing?
Watering her toes.

Where is Penny?
Penny's on the ground.

What is Penny doing?
Rolling all around.

Now where is Lizzie?
With Penny in the tub,

Splashing and shouting
Rub-a-dub-dub.

Now where is Penny?
Turning on the hose.

And what is Lizzie doing?
Watering their clothes.